Rosie and Rasmus

written and illustrated by
SERENA GEDDES

ALADDIN
New York   London   Toronto   Sydney   New Delhi

ALADDIN

An imprint of Simon & Schuster Children's Publishing Division

1230 Avenue of the Americas, New York, New York 10020

First Aladdin hardcover edition April 2019

Copyright © 2019 by Serena Geddes

For information about special discounts for bulk purchases, please contact Simon & Schuster Special Sales at 1-866-506-1949 or business@simonandschuster.com.

The Simon & Schuster Speakers Bureau can bring authors to your live event. For more information or to book an event contact the Simon & Schuster Speakers Bureau at 1-866-248-3049 or visit our website at www.simonspeakers.com.

Book designed by Laura Lyn DiSiena

The illustrations for this book were rendered in watercolor.

The text of this book was set in Janson and Quimbly.

Manufactured in China 0119 SCP

10 9 8 7 6 5 4 3 2 1

Library of Congress Control Number 2018945164

ISBN 978-1-4814-9874-6 (hc)

ISBN 978-1-4814-9875-3 (eBook)

This is Rosie.

She lives in a little village with cobblestone streets, a water fountain, and an ice cream stand.

Every day Rosie watches and wishes.

She watches as the others play.

She wishes someone would see her.

This is Rasmus.

He lives in the big tree on top of the hill next to the
ocean that overlooks a little village with cobblestone
streets, a water fountain, and an ice cream stand.

Every day Rasmus watches and wishes.

He watches the birds dance in the sky.

He wishes he had wings so that he could fly.

Rosie shows Rasmus how to drink tea like a queen,

how to do a pirouette,

and how to jump rope.

And Rasmus shows Rosie
his kite, which flies,

his balloons, which float, and . . .

his favorite book, about
a dragon who soars
high in the sky.

And the dragon
saved the ship from
the raging storm.

Each day Rosie would work on a new plan to help Rasmus.
And together . . .

they would try . . .

and try . . .

and try new ways to fly.

But none of them worked, until . . .

Rosie gave Rasmus a gift.

But now, under the big tree on top of the hill . . .

Rosie and Rasmus must say farewell.

Rosie lives in a little village with cobblestone streets,
a water fountain, and an ice cream stand.

Every day Rosie watches other children play.

Every day . . .

but today.